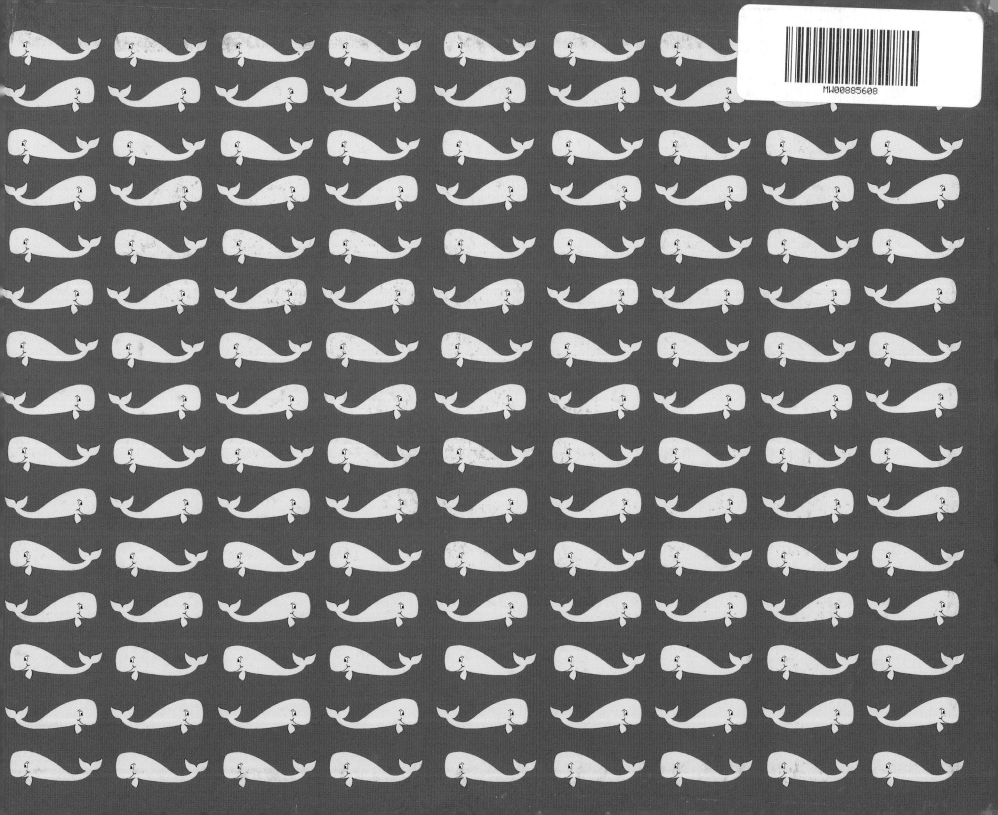

To my wife, Margi

Flag Football With Tuckey the Nantucket Whale®

Copyright ©2020 by Robert Cameron

Library of Congress Control Number: 2019914880

PRTWP1119A

Printed in Malaysia

ISBN-13: 978-1-64543-067-4

www.mascotbooks.com

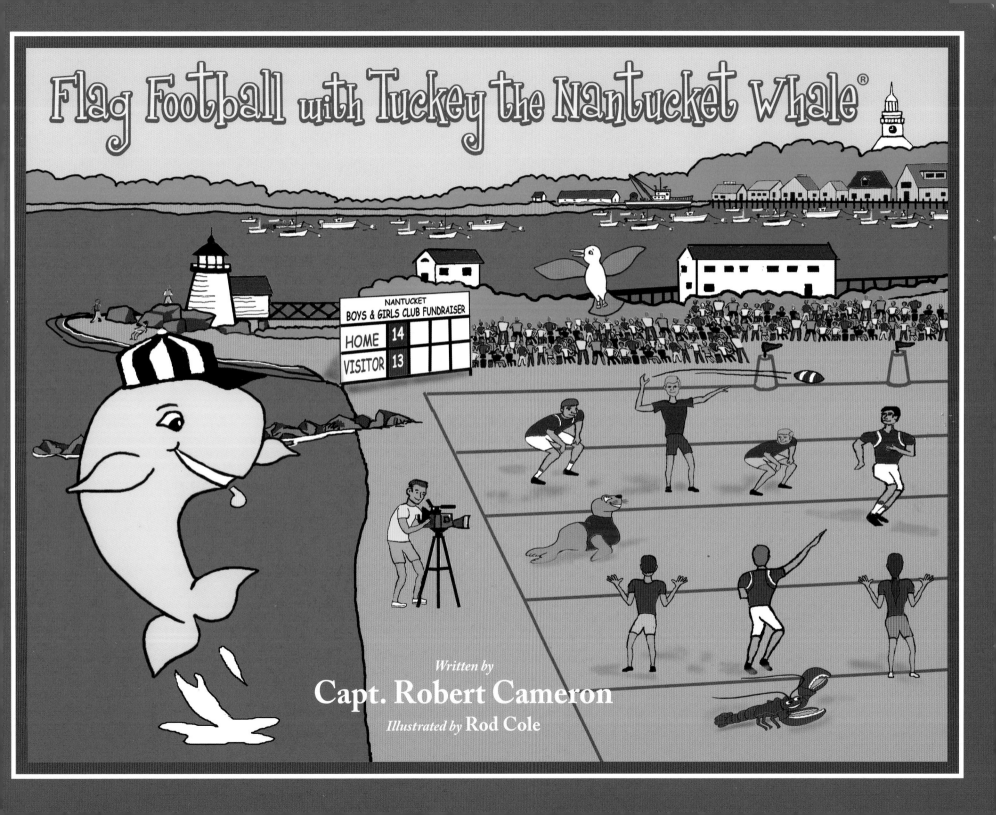

Great Britain

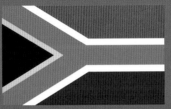
South Africa

Tanzania

U.S.A.

United Arab Emirates

Peru

South Korea

Singapore

Panama

Tuckey had a great time traveling around the world and learning about the people and cultures from 16 different countries. But now he's glad to be home again in the Nantucket waters. He loved reading his travel journal to the children on the lawn at the Nantucket Book Festival. Now he's ready to kick back and have some fun with his best buddies! Woo-hoo!

India

Malaysia

Australia

Philippines

China

Japan

Indonesia

Tuckey's friend Jakob got a new football for Christmas. Tuckey, Jakob, and their friends are having a catch at Jetties Beach.

Jakob yells to Nathan to go for a long pass. Mr. Lobster and Sammy the Seal double team him to keep him from catching the ball. But Nathan manages to snag it out of the air.

"Great catch, Nathan!" says Tuckey. "That gives me an idea. Why don't we have a game of flag football?"

Nathan, Jakob, and Sammy head over to the Weezie Library for Children. Sammy smiles as he passes a few Tuckey books on the front desk. It doesn't take long before Nathan finds a book called *Fundraising*.

At Jetties Beach, they read the book together and make note of all the things they have to do. Mr. Lobster lists these items on a whiteboard.

- DATE, TIME, AND PLACE
- APPROVAL
- WHAT CAUSE WE'LL BE SUPPORTING
- HOW TO SPREAD THE WORD
- PLAYERS AND VOLUNTEERS
- FOOD VENDORS
- TRANSPORTATION FOR FANS

FUND RAISING

Tuckey and his friends have agreed that they'd like the flag football game to support the local Boys & Girls Club. They plan on buying flag football uniforms and equipment. This year, the Nantucket Boys & Girls Club is transitioning one program completely to flag football. Today, over 1.5 million children in the U.S.A. play flag football. It is one of the fastest growing sports for children.

So now, they get busy making signs, posters, and advertisements for the event. They hang them all over the island in store windows, outside on poles, and in the windows of the Whaling Museum Gift Shop, Mitchell's Book Corner, Young's Bicycle Shop, The Hub, Murray's Toggery Shop, and 'Sconset Market.

Mr. Lobster is in charge of recruiting players and volunteers. He knows he, Sammy, Jakob, and Nathan will be playing, but there are five to seven players per team. They'll need at least six more.

The volunteers will help set up the event, make sure it runs smoothly, and clean up afterwards.

Mr. Lobster makes a sign-up sheet for players and one for volunteers. He posts them where everyone can see.

Nathan's role is to be sure there will be food at the event. He goes to a few of the local favorite restaurants. Something Natural says they'll bring sandwiches, water, and soft drinks.

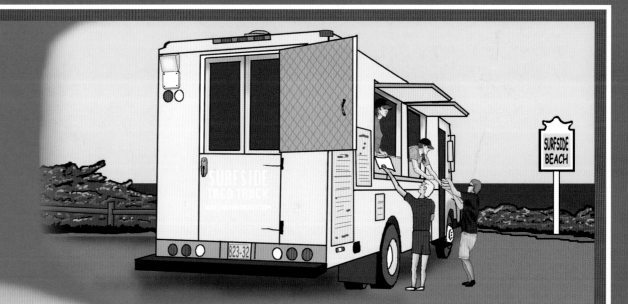

Surfside Taco Truck says they'll be there too. The Sandbar at Jetties Beach Grill has outside seating overlooking the beach where the game will be played.

Sammy is in charge of organizing transportation from 'Sconset. It is at the east end of the island. The game will be about 7 miles away. He talks with the local bus company. He wants to arrange a special bus that will go back and forth, making multiple trips out to the 'Sconset Rotary.

Later that day, Tuckey is swimming in the 'Sconset waters. He sees Super Bowl Champion Head Coach Bill Belichick of the New England Patriots. He was walking his Alaskan Klee Kai dog, Nike, down the beach. Tuckey gives him a big wave and stops to tell him about the flag football fundraiser game. Tuckey tells him that it would be an honor to have him there for the opening coin toss. He hopes he can make it!

Before they know it, it's game day! There's so much to do to get ready. First, they need to make the football field in the sand on the beach. A flag football field is much smaller than a regular football field. It is less than half the size, so it shouldn't take too long to mark out the lines. But how are they going to do it?

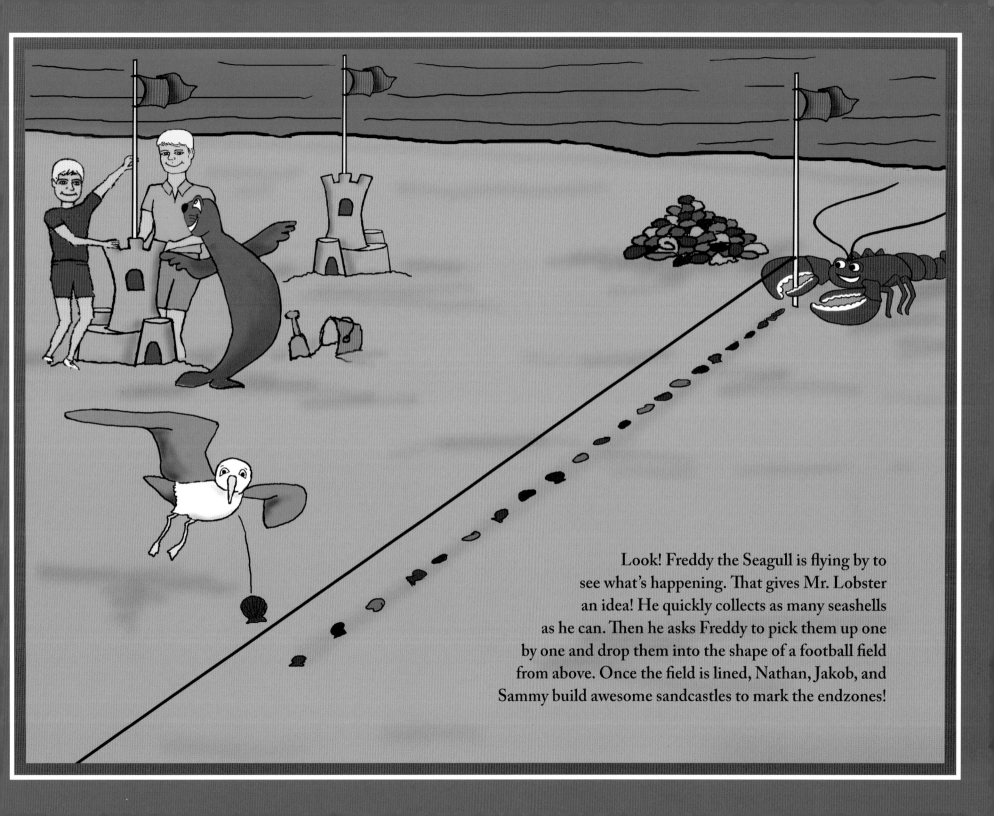

Look! Freddy the Seagull is flying by to see what's happening. That gives Mr. Lobster an idea! He quickly collects as many seashells as he can. Then he asks Freddy to pick them up one by one and drop them into the shape of a football field from above. Once the field is lined, Nathan, Jakob, and Sammy build awesome sandcastles to mark the endzones!

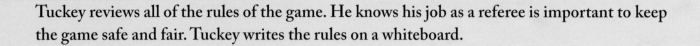

Tuckey reviews all of the rules of the game. He knows his job as a referee is important to keep the game safe and fair. Tuckey writes the rules on a whiteboard.

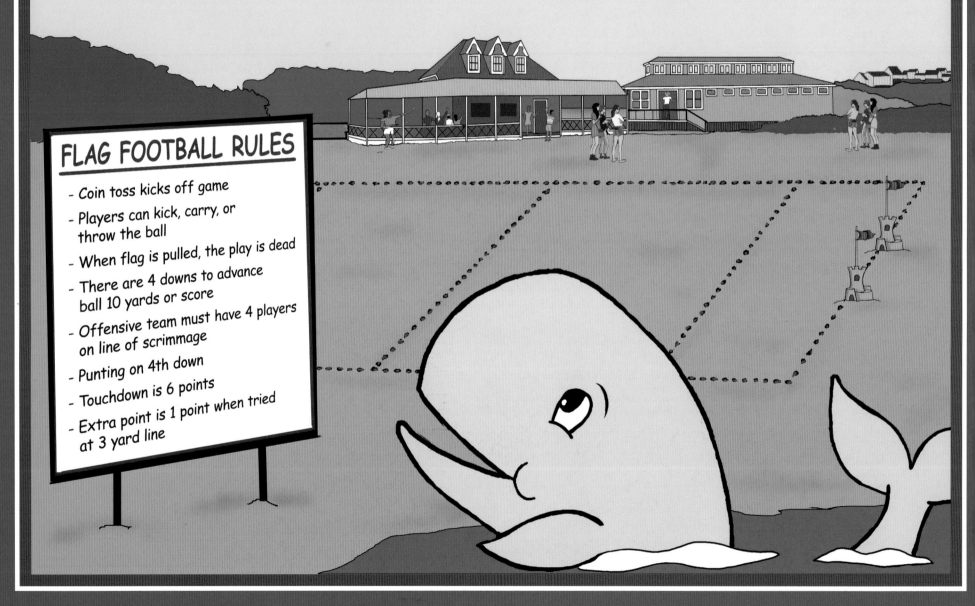

FLAG FOOTBALL RULES

- Coin toss kicks off game
- Players can kick, carry, or throw the ball
- When flag is pulled, the play is dead
- There are 4 downs to advance ball 10 yards or score
- Offensive team must have 4 players on line of scrimmage
- Punting on 4th down
- Touchdown is 6 points
- Extra point is 1 point when tried at 3 yard line

The game is due to start in a few hours, and Tuckey is anxiously awaiting the arrival of the players, volunteers, and fans. Suddenly, a fog rolls in from the ocean onto the beach. "Oh no," says Tuckey. "How will we be able to play the game? We won't be able to see the football!"

"Don't worry," says Freddy the Seagull. "I'll fly out and see how thick the fog is and the direction it is moving."

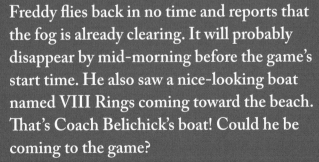

Freddy flies back in no time and reports that the fog is already clearing. It will probably disappear by mid-morning before the game's start time. He also saw a nice-looking boat named VIII Rings coming toward the beach. That's Coach Belichick's boat! Could he be coming to the game?

The players, volunteers, and fans begin to arrive. Some even come from Cape Cod and Martha's Vineyard to support this wonderful cause. Sammy's ocean friends are here to join the game too! Tuckey names the teams.

CAPE COD

MARTHA'S VINEYARD

NANTUCKET

FLAG FOOTBALL TEAMS

RED TEAM	BLUE TEAM
JAKOB - CAPTAIN	NATHAN - CAPTAIN
CLAW THE CRAB	MR. LOBSTER
SUNNY THE STARFISH	ALEYSIA
JET THE OCTOPUS	SAMMY THE SEAL
LIZZY	WHOA THE SEAHORSE

Tuckey is ready to get the game started. He blows his whistle and calls for the captains. Jakob and Nathan meet at midfield and shake hands. Just as Tuckey is about to flip the coin, Coach Belichick shows up on the field. What an honor!

Coach Belichick flips the coin high in the air, and Jakob yells, "Heads!"

"Heads, it is," says Coach Belichick. "Red Team, you will start with the ball."

Nathan and the Blue Team kick the ball off, and it soars through the air and lands in Lizzy's open arms. She runs the ball to the 40-yard line. Then Aleysia pulls her flag from her belt, and Tuckey blows his whistle to end the play. Nice run back by Lizzy!

For the Red Team's first play, quarterback Jet the Octopus throws a long pass to his receiver, Jakob. Jakob stretches his hands high and grabs the ball right out of the air. Wow, what a catch! He takes off running to the endzone. No one comes close to pulling his flags.

TOUCHDOWN!

What a way to start the game. The crowd goes wild, and the mermaid cheerleaders shout out their cheer!

Now Nathan and the Blue Team have the ball for the next series of plays. Nathan throws a short pass up the middle to Sammy the Seal. He makes a nice catch and starts running up the field. Unfortunately, his fins are wet and slippery, so the ball slips out. Oh no! Fumble! The Red Team's Claw the Crab recovers the ball. This is the first turnover of the game.

Jakob and the Red Team have the ball. Quarterback Jet throws the ball deep to Lizzy. Lizzy slips and falls, allowing Aleysia to intercept the ball.

She maneuvers her way through the Red Team and down the sidelines until she makes it to the endzone. Touchdown Blue Team! They attempt an extra point at the 3-yard line, but fail to make it. Will this cost them later on in the game?

There's nonstop action until Tuckey blows the whistle for halftime.

"Great half, everyone!" says Tuckey. "The score is 7 to 6, with Jakob and the Red Team leading. Remember to drink lots of water during halftime to hydrate."

Just before the second half is about to start, there is a big surprise. Two football players from the Super Bowl-winning New England Patriots show up for the game! They were visiting Nantucket. They heard about the game and fundraiser, and they want to play!

They high five everyone as they make their way to the field, and of course stop to say hi to Coach Belichick. Tuckey puts one Patriots player on each team. After they draw some plays in the sand, Tuckey blows the whistle to start the half. Everyone cheers loudly and is so excited to see them play. More and more people come to watch until it is standing room only. It's like the Super Bowl of flag football!

The second half continues with a lot of action. The Patriots player on the Red Team has the ball. He pretends to run the ball up the field, but instead tosses it to Jakob. A trick play! Jakob takes the ball all the way to the endzone for a touchdown. Great play!

Now Jakob's team is going for the extra point. They call a short down and out play to Lizzy at the 3 yard line for a successful extra point!

Now the Patriots player on the Blue Team has the ball. He hands the ball off to Nathan. Nathan runs right up the middle. It looks like one of his flags is about to be pulled, but he does a spin move around the defense covering him, breaks free, and runs to the endzone! Another touchdown, and another successful extra point!

The score is now Red Team 14, Blue Team 13. It's a close one, and there are only minutes left to play!

Just as the game comes to a close, a small plane flies over the field with a banner for the Boys & Girls Club. Pretty cool! The Red Team has won this game, but the Blue Team played well too. If only they had made that extra point! The Patriots players had a great time playing and even sign a few autographs with Coach Belichick.

Lots of fans and volunteers stay to clean the beach after the game. Tuckey and a few others count the money raised for the Boys & Girls Club. They made $2,655! Wow!

It has been a great day! So much fun and excitement, and all for a good cause!

A few weeks later, Tuckey and his friends attend the Tim Russert Summer Groove Boys & Girls Club event. It's one of the biggest summer fundraising events on the island! They have a great time dancing the night away to the fun music. But the best part of the night is when Tuckey and his friends present the check to the Boys & Girls Club. This will help them to get uniforms, equipment, and belts for flag football. Tuckey and his friends are so proud of what they've done to help the Boys & Girls Club. They are already planning the next flag football fundraiser game! Woo-hoo!

Here are some fun flag football facts from Tuckey!

- Super Bowl Champion Quarterback Tom Brady started playing flag football in elementary school and continued until starting his first year of high school.

- The longest continuous flag football game was 62 hours, 4 minutes, and 53 seconds. The game lasted from April 30th to May 3rd in 2015.

- The first organized flag football game was played in the 1930s.

- Flag football is played by both boys and girls from ages 5 to 17.

- Flag football is played internationally.

- The first ever National Collegiate Flag Football Championship was held at the University of New Orleans in 1979.

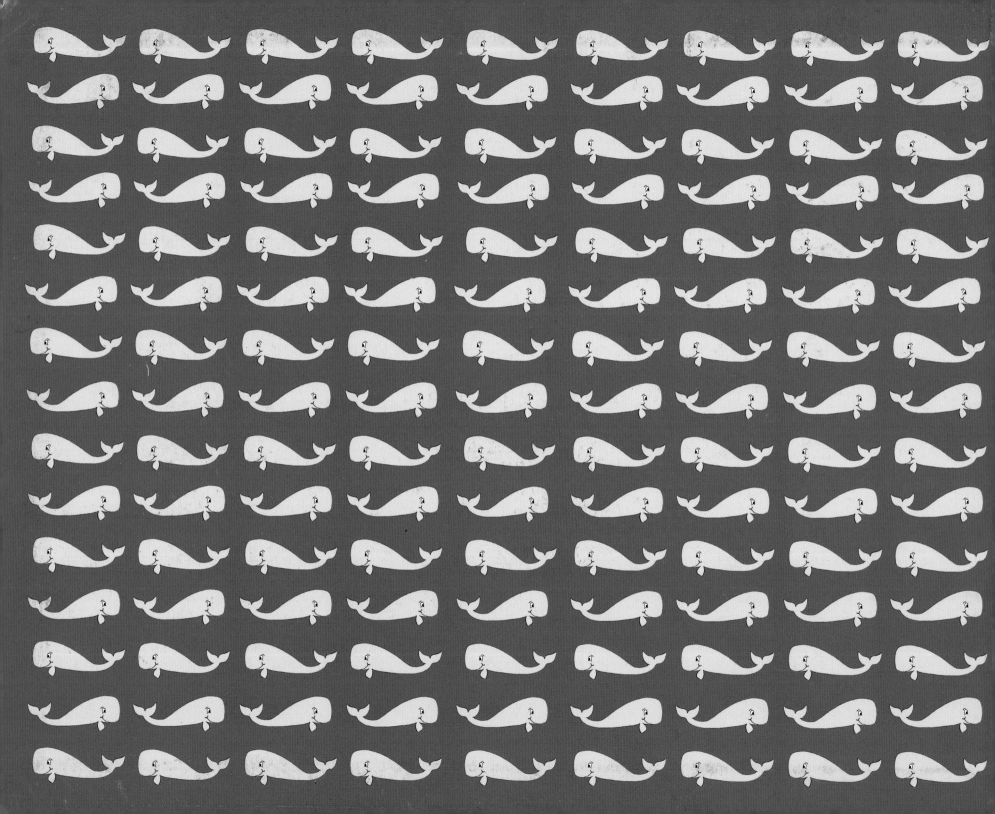